Disney
Winnie the Pooh

What Good Are Bugs?

BUGS
GO
PLEASE

It was a warm summer day in the Hundred-Acre Wood.
Butterflies were flitting here and there, ants were
marching in a row, and there wasn't a cloud in the sky.

Roo was jumping with the grasshoppers.

"Mama, look at me! I can jump just like
the grasshoppers," he said.

"That's very nice," said Kanga. "Now come, dear. It's the perfect day for a picnic."

"Did I hear someone say picnic?" asked Tigger, bouncing by. "Tiggers love picnics!"

"Hello, Tigger," said Kanga. "Perhaps you and Roo can bounce along and invite everyone to join us."

When they returned, Kanga had spread out a blanket and was getting things ready for the picnic.

"Everyone is coming, Mama," said Roo excitedly. "Except Owl—we couldn't get him to wake up! And Rabbit—he's going to be late."

Soon, the friends began arriving. Pooh brought a big pot of honey. Piglet brought some berries. And Eeyore brought some thistles.

"It's all I had," said Eeyore. "They're not bad if you chew 'em with your eyes closed."

Everyone sat down to a delicious lunch.

"I'll have a little larger helping, please," Pooh said to Kanga who was serving the honey.

When Pooh looked down, his honey was covered with ants! Pooh tried to shoo them away, but they just paraded across his plate, carrying his precious honey away, drop by drop.

"Zzz-zzz!" Swish! "Zzz-zzz!" Swish!

Pooh looked over at Eeyore. He was surrounded by gnats. His ears twitched and his tail swatted, but the gnats kept swarming.

"I suppose I should be thankful they're noticin' me," said Eeyore gloomily.

Bzz! Zip! Click! Clap! There were bugs everywhere! Flies were landing on the sandwiches; grasshoppers were leaping high and low; and mosquitoes were buzzing in Roo's ears.

"Mama, there's a tickly in my ear," said Roo.

"And there's an itchy on my arm," said Pooh.

"Yeech! Buddy Bear, what's that smell?" asked Tigger, holding his nose.

"Stink, stink, stink," said Pooh.

"Tiggers don't like stink bugs!" cried Tigger.

Meanwhile Pooh's tummy was getting rumblier and grumblier. "Let's go to my house for an *indoor* picnic," he suggested.

When they got to Pooh's house, a swarm of angry bees chased them away.
Tigger looked up and saw a honeypot hanging down from the beehive.
"Seems the bees don't like your new honey-catching invention, Pooh
Boy," he said.

Pooh and his friends ran to Owl's house.

"Owl, we need your help," Pooh called.

"The skeetos are buzzing in my ear," said Roo.

"Can you please get the bugs to stop *bugging* us?" asked Tigger.

Eeyore swung his tail to swat away the gnats, and it fell off.

"Seems things would be nicer without 'em," said Eeyore as Kanga helped put his tail back on. "What good are bugs anyway?"

Owl tried to listen, but he could barely keep his eyes open.

"I'm sorry," he said, "could you repeat that? I'm a bit tired. A chirping cricket has been making so much noise around here lately, I've hardly slept a wink."

"They're tickly!" said Roo.
"They're icky!" said Eeyore.
"They're stinky!" said Tigger.
"They're s-s-scary," said Piglet.
"And they eat honey!" Pooh added.

A meeting was called at Pooh's Thinking Spot
to figure out how to get rid of the bugs.
"We could make a sign," said Pooh. "But it will
have to be big enough for all the bugs to read."

Piglet ran to get Christopher Robin's help with their sign.
As Piglet ran out, Rabbit ran in.
"Sorry, I'm late," he said. "My garden is filled with caterpillars. I had to walk carefully, so I wouldn't step on them."

"Bugs can certainly be a bother," said Pooh.
"That's why we're asking them to go away!" said Roo.

"Go away?" Rabbit asked. "Well, I don't know about that. They've always been in my garden." He paced back and forth nervously. Rabbit wasn't sure, but he had a feeling his garden needed the bugs. "Maybe my garden likes bugs."

"*Likes* bugs?" asked Pooh. "Well, perhaps we should go ask your garden why."

When everyone got to Rabbit's garden, it was overflowing with colorful fruits, vegetables—and bugs.

"Let's look closely and see what they're doing," said Rabbit.

Everyone crouched down in the dirt to watch the bugs.

"The ants are making the soil soft so my vegetables can grow," said Rabbit. "And these little animals called earthworms are leaving deposits that make the soil richer."

"What about these crawlin', crunchin' caterpillars?" asked Tigger.

"Caterpillars grow into butterflies," said Rabbit. "And some butterflies help fruits and flowers grow by spreading powdery yellow grains called pollen that help plants make seeds."

Soon, Christopher Robin joined them.

"I made the sign Piglet asked for, but are you sure you want the bees to go away, Pooh?" he asked.

"Hmm, where there are bees, there is honey…so the bees can stay!" Pooh decided.

BUGS
GO
PLEASE

"If the grasshoppers go, you won't get to hop with them anymore,"
Kanga reminded Roo.

"But I like jumping like the grasshoppers," Roo said proudly. "I want
the grasshoppers to stay!"

Rabbit really thought hard about how important bugs were.
"And if the ants go, the soil in my garden will be hard as a rock. If the butterflies and bees go, my flowers won't grow...."

"Lots of bugs are useful," said Christopher Robin. "We need bugs—even when they seem bothersome."

Pooh and his friends decided that the Hundred-Acre Wood was a better place *with* bugs. With Christopher Robin's help, they took the sign and crossed out "go," and replaced it with "stay." Now instead of the sign saying "Bugs Go Please!" it said, "Bugs Stay Please."

Then Pooh dribbled a bit of honey on the sign. "Just a smackerel," he said, "for the bugs!"

Go Buggy!

If we didn't have bugs in the world, we would have no honey, apples, grapes, clover, cotton, and fewer garden vegetables, too. All these plants depend on insects to pollinate their flowers and help them grow. Some insects can stop other bugs from destroying our farmers' crops. And all bugs help maintain nature's delicate balance.

Young children learn about the world through hands-on activities, observing, questioning, describing, and creating. Help your child learn more about bugs with these fun, simple activities.

Art Activity:

Draw a picture of one of the flowers in the garden. Be sure to include at least two of the insects in the garden that help make that flower grow.

Bug Observation:

Step 1: Go outside to a flower garden. Bring a magnifying glass, some paper, and crayons.

Step 2: Look at the dirt. What kinds of bugs are living there?

Step 3: Look at the grass and other plants. What kinds of bugs are there?

Step 4: Look at the flowers. Do you see bees or butterflies?

Step 5: Use the magnifying glass to get an up-close view of the bugs that are busy working in the garden. (Be careful, however, *not* to magnify sunlight onto the bugs.) In one way or another, they are all helping the garden grow.